WHEN THE
FOG
ROLLS IN

PAM FONG

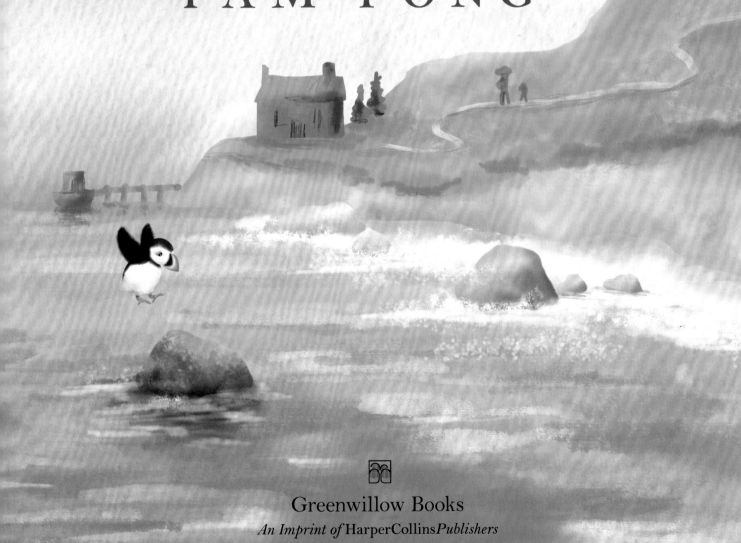

Greenwillow Books

An Imprint of HarperCollinsPublishers

On a clear day, it's easy to see your way.

You can just take flight.

But sometimes,

the fog rolls in.

It may be thin at first,

but it can grow

thicker

and

thicker . . .

until everything is fog.

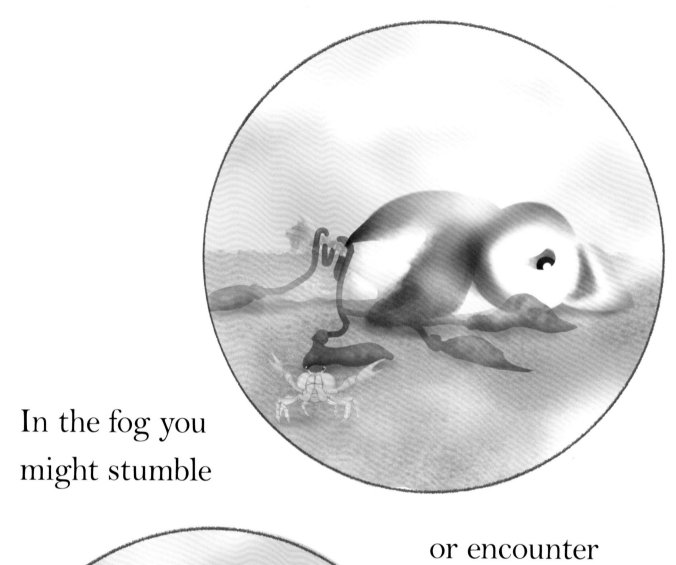

In the fog you
might stumble

or encounter
the unexpected.

It's easy to be confused

and hard to find your way out.

Puffin Point

So you

might

stay

right where you are.

But staying still does not clear the fog.

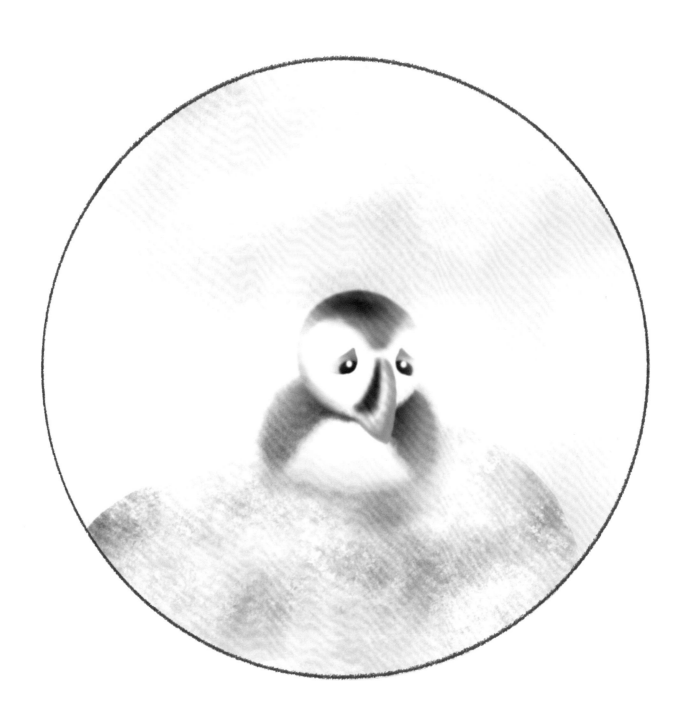

Sometimes, it can even be . . .

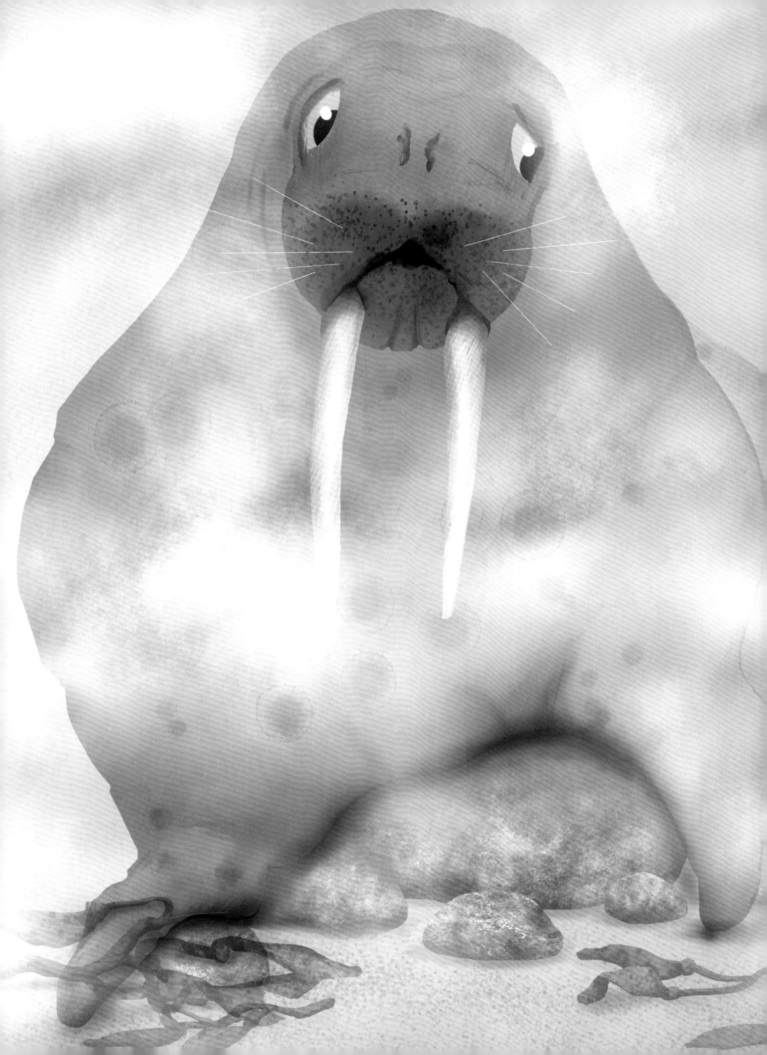

DANGEROUS!

If you want to escape the fog,

the best way to go

is directly through it.

Move in for a closer look.

Because the closer you get,
the more you will see.

And the more you see,

the clearer the path becomes.

Soon, the fog will lift and you will find . . .

a bigger world
    has always been there,
        waiting for you.

For all who seek
understanding
and truth

When the Fog Rolls In
Copyright © 2023 by Pam Fong
All rights reserved. Manufactured in Italy.
For information address HarperCollins Children's Books,
a division of HarperCollins Publishers,
195 Broadway, New York, NY 10007.
www.harpercollinschildrens.com

Full-colored artwork was created with watercolors
and compiled digitally using Adobe Photoshop.
The text type is 26-point Bell MT Std.

Library of Congress Cataloging-in-Publication Data is available.

ISBN 978-0-06-313654-0 (hardcover)

First Edition

23 24 25 26 27 RTLO 10 9 8 7 6 5 4 3 2 1

Greenwillow Books